THE GATE

A Tale for the 21st Century

THE GATE

A Tale for the 21st Century

E. Johannes Soltermann

SunShine Press Publications

SunShine Press Publications, Inc.
P. O. Box 333
Hygiene, CO 80533-0333 ; U.S.A.
Web Site: *www.sunshinepress.com*

Cover design: Bob Schram of Bookends
Cover and book illustrations: E. Johannes Soltermann
Book design: Jackie Hofer of SunShine Press Publications

Publisher's Cataloging-in-Publication Data

Soltermann, E. Johannes
    The gate: a tale for the 21st century.
    p. cm.
    ISBN: 1-888604-09-3
    I. Title
PZ4.B121 1999   813'.5'4
                                       99-60155

This book has been taken, entirely and directly, from the Universal Lifestream which is Spirit. It is not in any way connected to outward earthly occurrences. Should you nevertheless find similarities between this book and yourself or other actual persons or places, I encourage you to attribute those similarities to either your vivid imagination or to your vast and enormously resplendent inner life.

Printed in the United States of America
Printed on recycled acid-free paper using soy-based ink

To every Soul on Earth

Contents

INTRODUCTION

L et me explain something: Ever since I came to the U.S.A. from Austria in 1992, the cashier in the grocery store, the cab driver, the hobo on Nicollet Street, my dentist, every single person I meet throws the question at me: "You have an ACCENT! Where are you FROM?"

Not everyone who asks is interested. We know that. Still, we all do it. You are bored. You haven't taken anybody for a ride yet today. Your boss told you to get lost to Antarctica, maybe they have a job for you there. You're just ready to take out your frustration on the first soul that comes along: "Hey, you have an ACCENT! Are you from Kurrekurredutt Island or something where they eat earthworms and worship armadillo droppings?"

I love people. Don't take me wrong. But I also care for myself. There are times when one needs protection.

9

So I finally shot back: "I am from GREENLAND!" That shut them up.

But something else happened. I heard a click in my head. And I felt commotion in my heart. A chunk of memory arose like some sunken continent from beneath the ocean of my subconscious: "GREENLAND! How much I love you! I know I lived on your lands long ago. My name was not Soltermann. And my hair was not blond. And even you looked different then!"

Thanks to all the individuals who had pestered me with this question, I now got in touch with an old, lost love. Instantly I knew what I had to do next: Rushing to my travel agent and buying a round-trip ticket. Destination: Of course, GREENLAND!

* * *

Touchdown in Nuuk, the capital. In the low south-west. High summer, August. Still, chilling cold. I was glad I had brought my coat.

I found a fishing boat that took me southwards, following the coastline. It seemed I should go that way. On the ninth day—I assume we had already passed Cape Farewell, the southern tip—the men beached the trawler in a cove between two high mountains.

Smiling, they motioned me to get off board and follow them inland. What we found, what I found—

they seemed to know the place very well—was an astonishingly lush valley with plenty of fruit trees, grasses, butterflies, deerlike animals, sparrows, and yes, even cucumbers! I jerked off my coat. It was hot!

Have you ever heard about hidden valleys in Tibet, enclaves with tropical climate? Like the one Lobsang Rampa describes in his book *The Third Eye?* I never believed those reports. But here I was, on the island of GREENLAND, a giant supposedly frozen 12 months out of the year, surrounded by birdsongs, abundant green, and teased by an almost Caribbean breeze.

We reached a group of small huts. People streamed out of them as we approached, short people with supernatural friendliness. Soaked up by awe I forgot to wonder as a couple invited me into their home. Inside the one-room-house three kids were squatting around a fireplace. Steaming food on large silver plates was waiting to be savored.

What I noticed about these fellows was that I couldn't figure out any difference between grown-ups and children, except their size. They all behaved the same. They played alike. They worked alike in the fields. No running around screaming, no scolding, no banging toys or stomping feet.

In the evenings when they sat together chatting, more

than once I closed my eyes and couldn't tell who was talking, a child or an adult. I would see little ones consoling elders. And I saw parents consulting their two-year-old.

On my sixth day of stay, the village turned excited. A farmer from higher up the valley came to "town." To trade products and to exchange news. All this I learned from a young woman, Meisha, who spoke English because she had been a scholarship student at Columbia University.

She also told me that the farmer wanted to meet with me. That was arranged, and the next day I sat with this ninety-year-old man in the shade of the big northern fir. Meisha translated as usual. She said he appreciates my effort to help him. I asked what he was talking about. He pulled a bundle of papers from his cloak and handed them to me with the words: "Thank you for showing this to the world!" And he beamed through his eyes like three suns in one.

I briefly looked down at what I held: coarse, hand-made sheets of paper, covered with hieroglyphics I could not decipher. He didn't seem to give me much choice. So I asked him: "What do you mean by 'showing to the world'?" He just waved his hand and whispered: "You know what to do." With that he got up, bowed, and disappeared.

I stayed another three weeks, tremendously enjoying

this unusual community. All my senses screamed: "I lived here before! And not surrounded by permafrost, but at another time. When the mile-thick icesheet still was distant future. When elephants and aurochs roamed the green hills that spanned all corners of this landmass."

* * *

Back home I went to the United States with gratitude in my backpack. And a stack of papers I had no clue yet what to do with. From Meisha I had learned that the writings were a blend of ancient Nordic and Asian tongues. The language the whole valley spoke. But she had never gotten around to translating what the farmer had written.

* * *

A year or so later, at a meeting of the Shakespeare Oxford Society in the public library of Concord, Vermont, I met a very nice, retired professor. He had taught paleontology at Vermont State University. Beside this duty, his lifelong passion had been to study hieroglyphics of the Phoenicians, the Atlanteans, and the different peoples of the Empire of Uighur in central Asia, then part of the even older Empire of the Sun, Mu.

Back at my office in Minneapolis, I sent Dr. Jeremiah Navratil laserprint copies of all the farmer's handwritings. He quickly responded with a gracious letter:

March 8, 1996   Hazelstead, VT

Dear Mr. Soltermann,

This is quite a find you have! I haven't seen such a good piece of discovery ever since I visited Kurdistan in 1956 to unearth some of the Naacal Scriptures. Let me assure you that I feel most honored that you chose to involve me in this translation. Let me also say that I am committed already for the next three months to a long-planned trip to Srinagar in Kashmir. Upon returning, I shall be happy to invest my time into translating your fascinating find.

Until then, my most kind regards,
Jeremiah Navratil

* * *

Three years passed. I tried to call him. I faxed him. I e-mailed. Nothing. Then suddenly I got a note in the mail. He apologized profoundly for the delay. He had been unable to reach me because he had been captured by rebels and held imprisoned for over two years: "... which gave me valuable time to study their language and their habits ... but I really would have liked to stay longer and do more research ...," he explained.

Only three months after that I received the complete translation. From the typeface alone I could tell that Dr. Navratil had put in his very best efforts. And his credentials as a linguist, I had learned in the meantime, are really, really impressive.

Well, the only credit I can claim for this book is, that I undertook the journey to Greenland. The rest seems pretty much out of my hands.

All that's left is to wish you HAPPY READING. I hope you feel enriched by the farmer's account.

E. Johannes Soltermann
—Editor

* * *

A final note:

Should you feel compelled to search for my beloved enclave, please, do not. The mere thought of it being overrun by tourists makes me sick. I strongly urge you to look for YOUR OWN "GREENLAND," a place where You are exceedingly happy.

Should you STILL want to find MY valley, I'd like you

to do so for the best reasons: Because you TRULY want to know who you are. Because you love every thistle as you love your own heart. Because you see yourself breathing in every swallow darting by, in every pop can rolling at your feet, in every sister, in every brother you embrace.

THE GATE

A Tale for the 21st Century

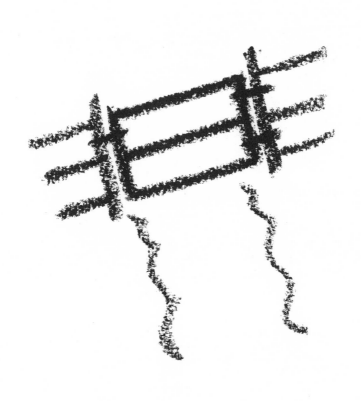

Here begins the mysterious manuscript that I have received on the island of Greenland from the hands of the farmer in early summer of 1995—as translated by Professor Jeremiah Navratil, Ph.D.:

Hello. I am a simple farmer on KALAALLIT NUNAAT (i.e., Greenland). I live in a valley that is not so well-known. We see few visitors here. And if I meet somebody, it is usually a hunter from further south who is pursuing some prey.

I haven't always lived here. But that is a different story. I traveled before I settled here.

Before I was born, my father wrote and sang songs for the king of QAANAAQ (i.e., Thule, a city on the northwestern coast of Greenland). That was long ago. When he settled and became father, and my sister and I were born, he had moved to QAQORTOQ (i.e., Julianehab, a city on the southwestern coast of Greenland) and had opened his own tannery. But in his spare time, he still wrote and sang songs. Not modern songs in the modern language, the one that the Danish and before them the Vikings had tried to impose on us.

No, my father sang THE OLD LANGUAGE, the language of the UIGHUR, a people long gone. I am saying this because you might wonder why a simple farmer like me can write. I learned it from my father. And like my father, I used to talk and write in WAVE-TONGUE. This is a way of speaking we learn from the waves of the sea. Our voice rides on the waves of our breath like a boat.

Many, many moons ago, when my legs were still quick and my heart was held captive by scars, I met a stranger here in this valley. He was unlike any other HUMAN I had ever met.

His visit lasted only from low-sun to sundown. One sunrise later, while my knees were still shaking from that experience, I sat down at our kitchen table and wrote on paper what I had heard, what I had seen and what I had thought during that one eventful day.

I wrote everything down in WAVE-TONGUE, and I started out with the stranger's own words:

Entrance

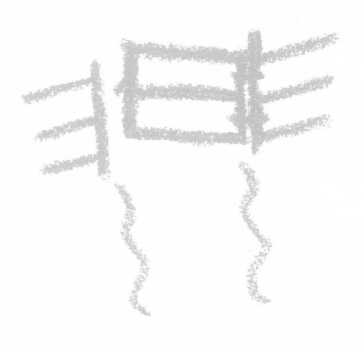

IMAGINE a landscape.
YOUR landscape.
It can be the one
you live in here.
Or another one,
whichever you choose.

IMAGINE the hills,
the mountains, the meadows,
the rocks, the valleys,
the seashore;
the glacier, the arid desert,
the field, the forest,
the lake.

IMAGINE that each
of the features you SEE
is a complete WORLD
of its own.

The forest is a WORLD of its own.
The plain is a WORLD of its own.
Every pond, every clearing
is an entire COSMOS.

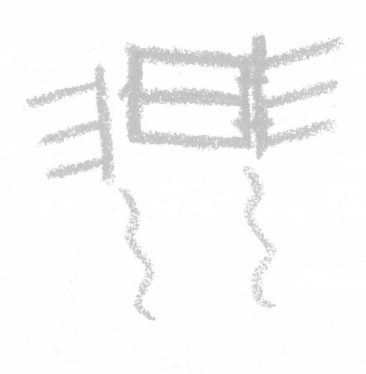

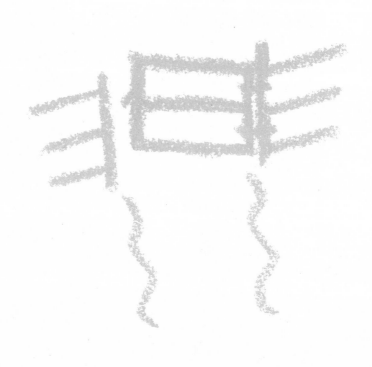

Remember, you are
completely FREE
to TRAVEL
wherever you like.

Cross the bridge,
delve into the thicket,
explore the patch
of linseed flowers.
Climb up Mount Threshmore.

IMAGINE your SELF venturing
eternally through INFINITE
WORLDS.

That is
how CREATION is set up,
you DREAMER, he said,
leaning his head.

Then he continued:
What are you doing
in this LIFE,
what is your purpose here?

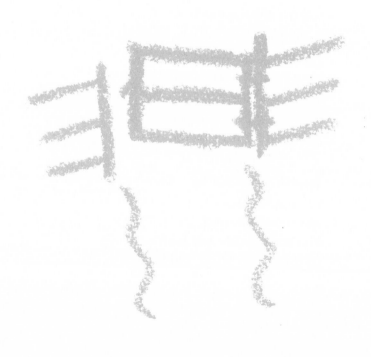

Remember, you are
completely FREE
to TRAVEL
wherever you like.

Cross the bridge,
delve into the thicket,
explore the patch
of linseed flowers.
Climb up Mount Threshmore.

IMAGINE your SELF venturing
eternally through INFINITE
WORLDS.

That is
how CREATION is set up,
you DREAMER, he said,
leaning his head.

Then he continued:
What are you doing
in this LIFE,
what is your purpose here?

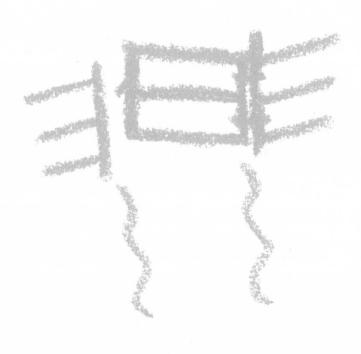

Any idea?

Oh my God,
he brought me to tears!
How should I know?
I, who left his mother,
I, who sold his father
to passing merchants
for a ride to Dinkytown.
Yes, Dinkytown,
where the girls smell so sweet
that you faint or weep.
Where you get lost
for just one fleeting look.

Yes, the man said,
**you must truly get lost
to find your REAL SELF.**

But how ...

Psst! his voice cut me short,
you must not speak for now!

So I was sitting quietly
on our dusty road,
facing this man
whom I trusted.
How I hated to trust him,
I don't trust anybody,
I'm too SACRED
to trust anybody.

You are right, he smiled,
you don't trust anybody.
And I will tell you why:

A long time ago
you were one of us,
traveling through all the WORLDS.
You rollicked about
like all SOULS in their JOY,
when they're FREE
in SPIRIT and THOUGHT.
But then you got caught
in the gravity of Earth,
and your rapid descent began.

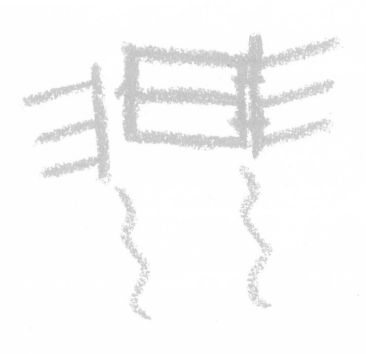

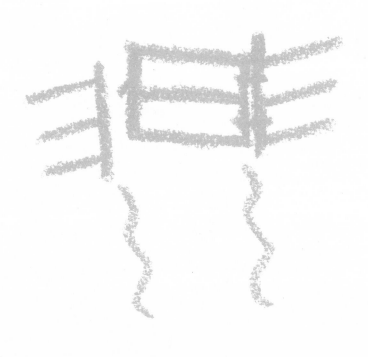

Why are you telling me this?
I shouted at him,
I just met you
a few breaths ago!
Do you think, just because
I am honest and friendly,
you can blab to me
whatever you like?

I didn't meet you
just a few breaths ago.
I have known you
ALL my LIFE, he replied.

I felt puzzled.
But for HEAVEN'S sake,
the man should at least
introduce himself!
Tell me right NOW
who he IS,
instead of misusing
my patience!

Okay,
the stranger once again

responded to my thoughts.
**Who do you think
guards your License To Heaven,
while you are retraining
to use it?**

I didn't feel like sitting anymore.
I jumped up,
on the spot.
Why are you telling me this!
I repeated, not knowing
what else to say.

I'd been shuffling home
from a hard day of work,
to my wife and my kids
on the farm.
Then this stranger emerged
from the empty horizon.
I couldn't help
dropping my bag.
So I stood there, waiting,
until he reached me,
my feet wouldn't walk away.

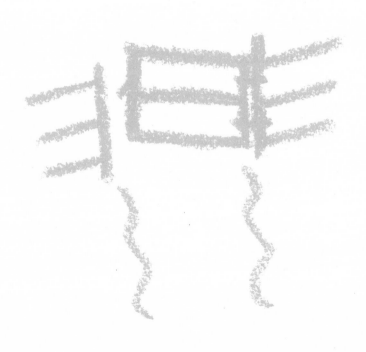

But I didn't plant crops
and build my own house
to waste time
on a conversation like that!
Why did I stand here?
Why was I interested
in talking to this fellow?
Foreigners come by,
once in a while,
but none as strange as this one!

The man's gray hair
touched his shoulders,
but he clearly looked
younger in his face.
As he stood directly
in front of me,
he was rather short,
yet taller than a child.

**I must be forty-six,
or sixty-four?
Or maybe even
four-thousand six-hundred?**

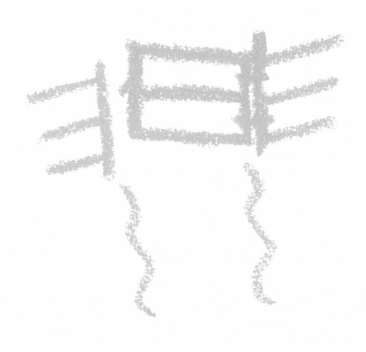

His roar of laughter
echoed through the valley,
the passage I TRAVEL daily.

I don't own a car,
I don't have a mule,
or a cart drawn by oxen.
But I do wear good shoes,
and they carry me well.
What more do I want?
I'm complete.

My name is HAROLD,
the man caught me off-guard,
his green coat open,
baring a brown suit.

My name is PRATTEN,
I lied to him,
trying to shake him off.

He burst into laughter
again and again,
until he settled down.

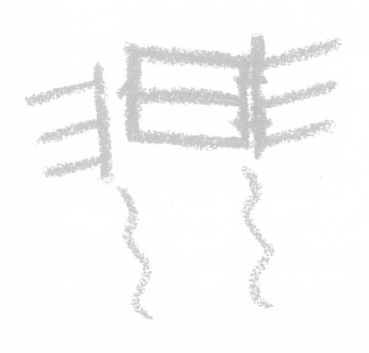

Let's face it, he resumed,
starting to walk
in my farm's direction,
**you ache to know
a lot of things.
But you still
don't have a clue.**

That's right! slipped
over my tongue,
although I wanted to hide it.

You agree, he continued,
**and do you know why?
Because** SOUL **knows it all.
And you, man, are** SOUL.

But the minister ...

Yes!
he cut me short again,
**you flock to church every week.
Yet the minister only
tells you what** HE **knows.
But** YOU **want to know**

47

the TRUTH!

I admit I liked him
a little bit.
Even though he spoke
this weird-fashioned.

So I addressed him:
Tell me something USUAL.
You know, how I talk
to my friends.
Something NORMAL,
can you talk
the NORMAL, REGULAR way?

You mean, the way
YOU say is NORMAL?
he beamed.

Yes, I nodded,
that's correct,
the way I say
is NORMAL.
Like, for instance,
what's your opinion

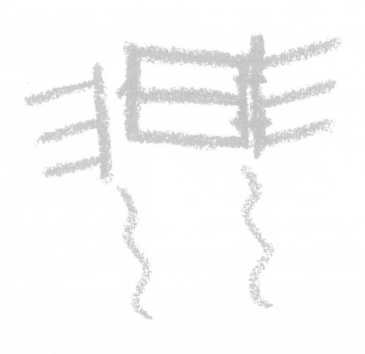

on the goat-cheese
I fermented yesterday?
I mixed plantain-juice
with twelve parts of milk.
What do you think
of this new combination?

Harold smiled
but answered nothing.
And I wondered why.

We walked side by side.

I usually don't like
people I never drank
tea with.

I value working
by myself in the woods.
Tilling the field,
watching the sunflowers
in years of abundant rain.

I tolerated his presence

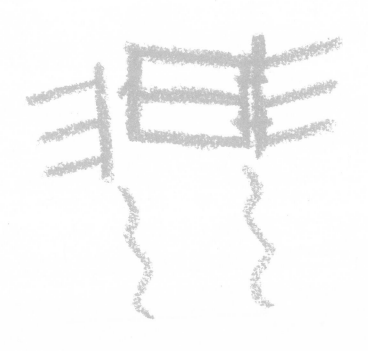

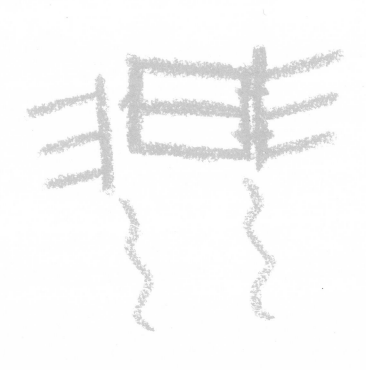

though I did not remember
permitting him
to break my SILENCE.

Then all of a sudden
he turned to the west
as if in a dance—
the SUN was just sinking
behind Mount Threshmore—
and he pointed his arm
straight ahead.

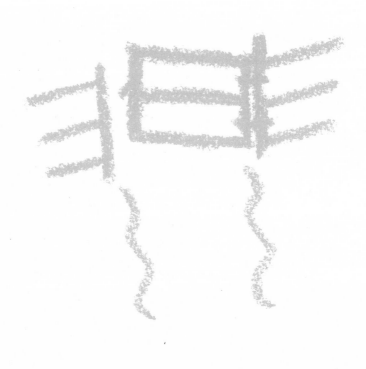

Passage

There it was.

A WHITE WHITE sheep.
I had never seen
an ALL-WHITE sheep.
We have BROWN sheep.
We have BLACK sheep.
But none like this
had I ever encountered.

It trotted down
the dimming slope,
gently moving towards us.
And for a reason
I cannot name
I expected it to
speak like a HUMAN.

It IS a HUMAN,
Harold remarked.
**But I turned it into a sheep,
so you can better**

relate to it.

I shook my head:
We have a story,
you know, I began,
a fairy tale about a man
who turns into a frog.
He once had promised
to help his neighbor
digging a well through rock.
He never showed up though,
that's why he got hexed …

But I don't believe
in fancies like that.
I think we are often
fooled into trusting
facts that do not exist.

In the meantime
the WHITE sheep
reached us and stood there,
a mere three feet away.

I could breathe
the smell of its wool.

And then it bleated.

I glanced at Harold.
Then laughter rolled
from my lips
because his HUMAN was
bleating like a lamb.
What did I tell you!
I yelled on and on,
I do not believe in
things nonexistent!

EXIT

This is the last scene
I remember
while I was still
in my regular mind.
In an instant
my vision blurred
and the sheep grew
to the size of MYSELF.
I could gaze into its eyes.

Next, the CREATURE
opened its mouth
and spit a whole STREAM
of GOLD coins.
At least a bucketful.
I saw them on the ground.
Not having drunk
one blighted drop of wine,
I was witnessing
this delusion.

NOW something pulled me
out of this MOMENT.

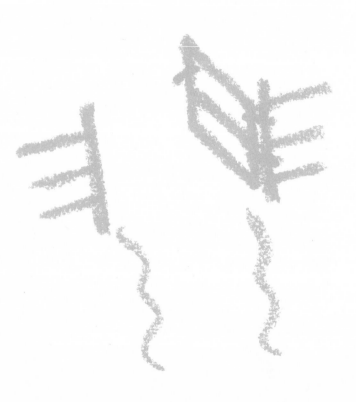

It was Harold,
patting my shoulder:
Let's leave from here.
You've got to go home.

I totally had
forgotten who I was;
or where I belonged.

That hour I changed
to a different person.
I could not reverse it.
Still NOW I AM
that same, different person
while giving you
this whole account.
My memory is fresh.
It was just yesterday
that it all happened to me.

Harold walked at my side.

I was glad this time.

I wasn't sure
what I was doing.

**So you don't believe
in fairy tales?**
he piercingly resounded.

No I don't, I gasped,
wanting to breathe.

**Then what do you make of
what you just watched?**
the stranger inquired to know.

I cannot say, I replied,
feeling truly shaky.

That sheep was YOU,
I heard him mutter ...

What?
I bellowed.
What did you say?

That sheep that spit
GOLDEN coins over there
was YOU, he repeated.

How can that be?
I was here—and it was there.
I'm only ONE, not TWO!

That's right, he calmed me.
I only showed you
who you ARE, you SEEKER.
Your mind's a sheep,
imitating your parents.
Always, always, always.
You have no idea
how big an impact
it has on a child
to imitate.
We are so vulnerable
to any influence.
Because we're open
to LOVE.

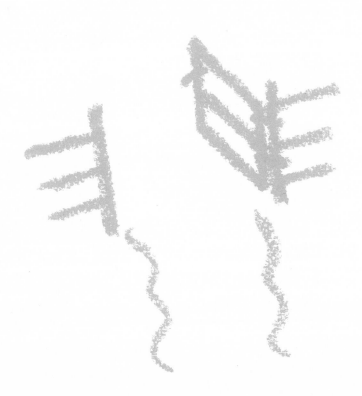

But what does this
have to do with me?
my strained lips quivered.

Wait,
his undisturbed voice
came on again,
I will tell you what:
We are all sheep,
until we grow tall enough
to become adept
in spitting GOLD.

What do you mean by
—GOLD? I asked.
Not because I wanted to know.
But because I very much
longed to bring
this meeting
to an end.

GOLD—

that is your SOUL,
my friend.
that's who you ARE,
ENTIRELY.

I'm SOUL anyway,
I snapped at him.
Why must you play
this theater then?

You SAY you're SOUL.
But REALIZING it
is quite a different matter.

I SEE.

You WANT to SEE.
But you haven't developed
your INNER SENSORS yet.
That's why I put on
this "theater" for you,

as you decide to call it.
I didn't play it
for personal pleasure.
I didn't play it
to haunt you either.

But YOU called ME,
whether you know it or not.

WHEN *did I call you?*
I felt I had to
argue with this guy.

You called me
two hundred years ago.
But this was only
your last call.

What?
I never considered
myself insane.
Wow, this man was able
to push me!

You are not insane,
he again responded
to my secret THOUGHT.
You're just perceiving NOW
the WORLD you look at
from a different angle.

But how about
the two hundred years?
I'm fifty-four by now,
and I am well,
thank you very much!

Yeah,
the stranger grinned,
you're in good shape.
But let me mention
one more thing:

You are living
in the BLISS
of ETERNITY, right
HERE and NOW.

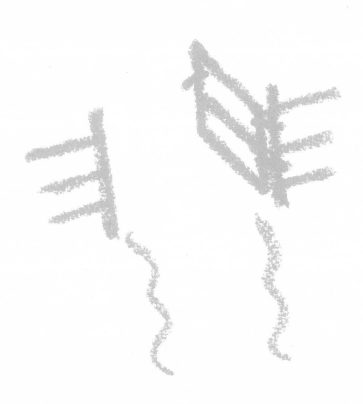

Every second of your LIFE.
But, just like
every SOUL out HERE,
you have the talent to forget.

Yet SOUL is strong.
That's why you
sold your father.
Your yearning to find out
who you ARE
was stronger than
what he had taught you.

He had taught you
to forget.
He had taught you
to hate your SELF.
That's what HIS father
had passed on to him:
Deny your SELF and adapt.

Your father was

a decent man;
he only could give
what he knew ...

Stop thinking
you are your MIND.
Stop thinking
you are your EMOTIONS.
Those viewpoints are
long out of date ...
Otherwise we wouldn't be
talking here ...

So, who ARE you?
I was tired,
as you can IMAGINE.
Thank HEAVENS I glimpsed
our gate in the dark.
and behind it the LIGHT
from the kitchen.
My wife must think
I'm lost or gone,

painfully crossed my mind.

I Am You,
rang this unmistakable
voice again,
triggering too many questions.

You are Not *in my body,*
or I couldn't look at you!
My impatience woke me
from fatigue.

That's true for Out Here,
the Physical World.
Although even that
could be changed.
But, if you ask me,
you better accept
the fulfillment
of your wish.

What did I wish?

93

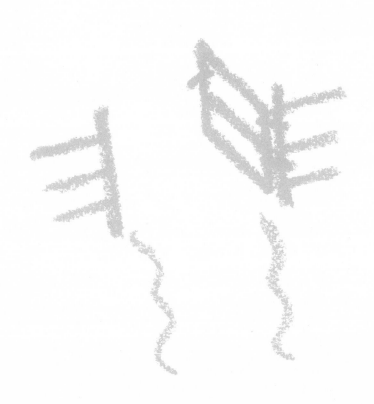

To know your SELF
ENTIRELY.
And that is
why I'm here.
To demonstrate to you
on familiar soil
what you are capable
of doing INSIDE.
Should I repeat my message?

WHAT *message?*

I reached the gate NOW,
thankfully leaning
my weight
against the beam.

The message I told you
right after we met
this afternoon.
You don't remember?

No.
Good.
Then I'll repeat it:

Regard every area
of your LIFE,
of your daily chores,
as a separate WORLD:
The field, the forest,
the lake, the mountain,
the valley, or your house.

These are all WORLDS,
complete in themselves,
yet distinct from each other.

You've got all these colorful
places OUT HERE
to train and remind you
of places INSIDE.
Visit them.

Close your eyes tonight
and believe you can BE
your REAL SELF again;
in its brightness,
fuller than ever.

And if you do so,
I will appear
in front of
your INNER VISION.

I will lead you through
the oceans, the doorways ...

You have to learn
to TRAVEL anew;
meadows and UNIVERSES,
my friend.

Because YOU are ME,
and I am YOU.

Today I teach YOU.
Next time YOU show ME!

Surrender to LOVE.

NOW, open the gate ...

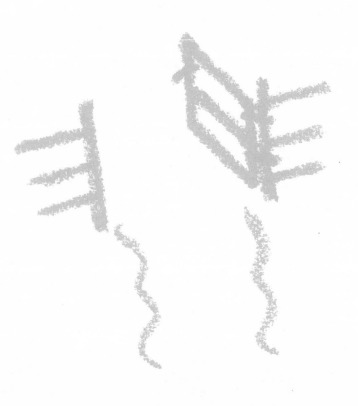

:These are the words I had heard from the stranger, the words I had spoken to him and the events that had taken place. On that one fateful day, many, many moons ago.

I am in the winter of my cycle now. I don't have the strength anymore to climb up Mount Threshmore, right to the edge of the glacier. But I won something instead. Every morning I rise, I see LIGHT flowing through me like water, whether the sun shines up in the sky or not. And every evening when I lie down to sleep, I see a smile coming from my INSIDE.

By night, when I wake up into a DREAM, I often lay eyes on the stranger as he is already waiting for me. We then TRAVEL together to WORLDS that are close to GOD'S HEARTBEAT. WORLDS where one is endlessly washed by LOVE.

More than I can say I have gained through being in touch with the stranger, who is no stranger to me anymore. In fact, if you would ask me to tell him apart from my very own

SOUL, I could not do so. I feel so deeply connected with him that I cannot say where he ends and I begin, or where I end and he begins.

These are the words I laid down on paper. Please accept them as my GIFT.

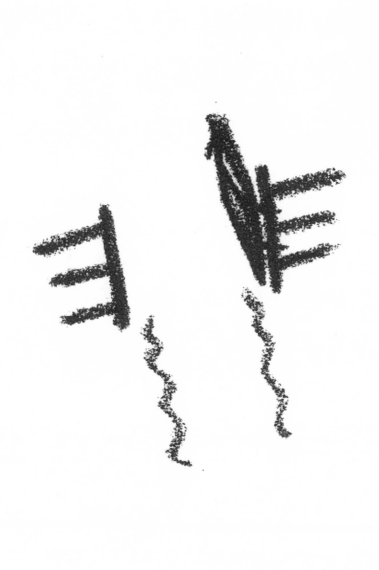

THE GATE is available through:

Bookstores: Local and national stores

Internet:
http://www.sunshinepress.com
http://www.barnesandnoble.com
http://www.borders.com
http://www.amazon.com
http://www.amazon.co.uk (England)
http://www.amazon.de (Germany)
http://www.consciousmedia.com

SunShine Press Publications, Inc.
P. O. Box 333
Hygiene, CO 80533-0333 ; U.S.A.

If you would like to contact the author:

E. Johannes Soltermann
P. O. Box 2194
Minneapolis, MN 55402-0194 ; U.S.A.

Website: http://www.soltermann.com

About the Author

E. Johannes Soltermann is a native of Austria. With a suitcase in one hand and faith in the other, he came to the U.S.A. in 1992.

His formal education includes the Austrian Medical School, two diplomas in therapeutic massage, and training in numerous spiritual disciplines.

Johannes creates art in many mediums: music, writing, woodsculpting and cartoons. His songs were aired on Austrian Radio. His unique sculptures were exhibited across Europe and the United States. His articles and poems appeared in dozens of books, magazines and newspapers in the German language as well as English.

He has traveled in many parts of the world to gain his inventive perspective. He has known wealth and poverty, has worn Lederhosen and sneakers. His most noted journey is a continuing one devoted to spiritual growth and creating beauty in the world.

Johannes lives with his wife in Minnesota.

Notes